INSIGHT PUBLICA®

INSIGHT PUBLICA®

Nadakkave, Kozhikode, Kerala
Tel:0495–4020666
www.insightpublica.com
e-mail: insightpublica@gmail.com

Visiting Grandpa

N. Nosov

Translated from the Russian by *Fainna Solasko*

Drawings by *I Semenov*

The Singing Rabbit

Eskimo Folk Tales

Adapted for Children by *G Menovshchikov*

Translated by *Anatoly Bilenko*

Drawings by *Tatyana Chursinova*

Why Tuppy Doesn't Chase Birds

Y Charushin

Insight Publica Facsimile Edition: July 2020

ISBN 978-93-90355-61-7

VISITING GRANDPA

N. Nosov

Translated from the Russian by ***Fainna Solasko***

Drawings by ***I Semenov***

(Page No. 6-22)

THE SINGING RABBIT

Eskimo Folk Tales

Adapted for Children by ***G Menovshchikov***

Translated by ***Anatoly Bilenko***

Drawings by ***Tatyana Chursinova***

(Page No. 23-36)

WHY TUPPY DOESN'T CHASE BIRDS

Y Charushin

(Page No. 36-48)

Those fantastic
Soviet Books Again

"All of us still have those fond memories of the books from the erstwhile Soviet Union, which were once extensively circulated here, in Kerala - books of fabulous tales, riveting scientific facts and enchanting illustrations which stole the readers' hearts. They left in us an indelible impression and an unforgettable reading experience. An experience still ever-green in us, Malayali diaspora.

As the Union got dissolved, those charming books of tales too vanished, turning them into cherished memories of nostalgia. Yet, readers have relentlessly been looking for those inimitable books. That was why we, the INSIGHT PUBLICA, published a few of them in the same mode. We are grateful and glad to say that readers whole-heartedly backed us in realizing the project.

During the execution of our mission, we could fathom the depth and breadth of a great nation's remarkable literary project. Those sublime Soviet stories traversed in translation into many a nation and many a language. Those books were ubiquitous-not as merchandise, but as products of culture.

The fantastic bolstering that INSIGHT PUBLICA could get is the impetus that drove us daringly to undertake the mission of reprinting and republishing those Soviet works in Indian languages.

You readers need not anymore be discontented with the scanned copies of these books. INSIGHT PUBLICA will help reach into your hands those very books with the same freshness and warmth.

Let us present you again those fantastic Soviet Stories with humility and pride."

Sumesh Insight

N. NOSOV

VISITING GRANDPA

Translated from the Russian by FAINNA SOLASKO
Drawings by I. SEMENOV

Shurik and I spent last summer visiting Grandpa. Shurik is my kid brother. I was seven and already at school, but he wasn't. Still, he never obeys me. Well, I don't care. The day we arrived we explored the yard, the sheds and the attic. I found an empty jam jar and an empty box of shoe polish. Shurik found an old door pull and a big galosh. Then we nearly had a fight over a fishing rod in the attic. I saw it first and shouted, "That's mine!"

Then Shurik saw it and he shouted, "It's mine!"

I grabbed one end, he grabbed the other and we pulled. I got so mad I yanked it hard and he tumbled over backwards. Then he said, "Who needs your old rod? I have my galosh."

"You can kiss your lovely galosh, but don't you dare touch my rod again."

I found a spade in the shed and went off to dig worms, for I had decided to go fishing. Shurik went to ask Grandma for some matches.

"What do you want them for?" she demanded.

"I want to make a fire in the yard. Then I'll put the galosh on top of the fire and when it melts it'll be rubber."

"What will you think of next! Why, you'll burn the house down if I don't keep an eye on you. No, my dear, don't even ask me for them. Children should

never play with matches. Imagine such mischief!"

So Shurik tied one end of a piece of string to the door pull and the other to his galosh. He marched up and down the yard, dragging the galosh along. When he came over to me and saw me digging for worms he said, "You're wasting your time. You won't catch anything anyway."

"Why not?"

"I'll put a spell on the fish."

"Don't scare me," I sneered.

I dug some worms, put them in a box and went off to the pond. The pond was behind the house, where the collective farm's gardens began. I put a worm on my hook, cast my line and sat down to wait for a bite.

Shurik crept on me. Suddenly, he began yelling at the top of his voice: *Be he alive, or be he dead, I'll grind his bones to make my bread!*

I decided not to say anything, because I knew that if I did, it would only make him shout louder. He finally got tired of shouting his evil spell and tossed his galosh into the water. Then he pulled it up by the string. Then he threw the galosh into the pond and tried hitting it with stones in order to sink it.

For a moment or two I didn't say a word. Then I hollered, "Get out of here! You've scared all my fish away!"

"You won't catch anything anyway. I

put a spell on them." And he tossed his galosh into the middle of the pond!

I jumped up and grabbed a stick. Shurik ran off, with the galosh dancing along crazily behind him. He was lucky I didn't catch him.

I went back to the pond and sat down to fish again. The sun was high overhead by then and I still hadn't had a single bite. What was wrong with those fish? I was so mad at Shurik I could have beat his brains out. I didn't believe in his spell, but I knew that if I came home empty-handed he'd laugh at me. I tried everything: casting far into the pond and close to the bank, sinking my hook deeper into the water, but nothing helped. Finally, I decided to go home. Besides, I was very hungry.

There was a great hammering at our gate.

When I got closer I saw it was Shurik, hammering the door pull to the gate. I don't know where he had got the hammer and nails. "Why are you nailing this here?"

He was happy to see me. "Ah, the fisherman's back! Where's your catch?" he asked and giggled.

"Why are you nailing this to the gate? There is a handle here."

"So what? Now there'll be two. In case one comes off."

When he was all through hammering he had one nail left. He couldn't decide what to do with it. At first, he wanted to drive it into the fence. Then he got a better idea. He held his galosh to the gate with the sole against the wood and nailed it there.

"What's that for?"

"Nothing special."

"That's stupid."

Then we saw Grandpa coming home for

lunch. Shurik was scared. He tried to pull the galosh off the gate, but it was nailed fast. Then he stood in front of it, to hide it from view. Grandpa came up to us and said, "Good for you, boys! You've got down to work your very first day. Whose idea was it to nail another handle to the gate?"

"Shurik's," I said.

Grandpa cleared his throat. "Well, now we'll have two handles on the gate, one higher up, the other lower down, so that when a very short person comes calling he can pull the bottom one." Then he noticed the galosh. "What's this?"

I snorted, knowing that Shurik was in for it. Shurik turned red. He didn't know what to say.

"What's this, a mailbox?" Grandpa asked. "If the mailman comes round and sees nobody's home he can put our letters in the galosh. That's a very clever idea."

"I thought of it myself."

"Indeed?"

"Honest!"

"Good for you."

All during lunch Grandpa kept telling Grandma what a smart fellow Shurik was.

"It's really amazing. We'd never have thought of it. Imagine, he nailed a galosh to the gate! I've been saying we needed a mailbox, but never got around to it."

"I can take a hint. I'll get us a mailbox," Grandma said. "Meanwhile, the galosh can serve as one."

After lunch Shurik ran off to the orchard. Grandpa said to me, "Shurik has really been busy this morning. I'm sure you were up to something, too, Kolya. You

might as well confess and make your Grandpa happy."

"I went fishing, but I didn't catch anything."

"Where'd you go?"

"To the pond."

"No wonder. They've just dug it. I don't even think there are frogs in it yet. I'll tell you what. You go down to the river. The current is fast under the wooden bridge. That's where you fish." Grandpa went back to work. I got my rod and said to Shurik:

"Let's go down to the river to fish."

"You're trying to make up to me, aren't you?"

"What for?"

"So I won't put any more spells on the fish."

"I couldn't care less."

I took my box of worms and the empty jam jar for my fish and set off. Shurik tagged along behind. When we got to the river I found a good spot near the bridge and cast my line.

Shurik stayed close to me, mumbling,

Be he alive, or be he dead,
I'll grind his bones to make my bread!

He'd be still for a few moments and then start up again.

Be he alive, or be he dead...

Suddenly, I had a bite. I yanked at the line. The fish glittered in the air, slipped off the hook and fell wriggling onto the grass at the very edge of the bank.

"Catch it!" Shurik yelled and threw himself

on the fish. It slipped away and was thrashing about at the water's edge. Shurik finally got hold of it. I filled the jar with water and he dropped the fish in.

"It's a perch," he said as he examined it. "I'm sure it is. See the lines on it? Can it be mine?"

"All right. We'll catch a lot more."

We fished for hours that day and caught six little perches, four gudgeons and one small ruff. On the way

ПОЧТА

home Shurik carried the jar of fish. He wouldn't let me hold it. He was so proud he never minded his galosh missing from the gate. There was a shiny green mailbox in its place.

"Who cares?" he said. "And anyway, the mailbox is nicer." Then he ran off to show Grandma the fish. She was very pleased.

After a while I said to Shurik, "See, your magic spell didn't work. It's not worth much, is it? And I don't believe in it."

"I don't either. You have to be real dumb to believe in magic. Or very old."

This made Grandma laugh, because she was very old, but she didn't believe in magic spells, either.

THE SINGING RABBIT

THE SINGING RABBIT

ESKIMO FOLK TALES

ADAPTED FOR CHILDREN BY G. MENOVSHCHIKOV

Translated by *Anatoly Bilenko*
Drawings by *Tatyana Chursinova*

HOW THE RAVEN AND THE OWL PAINTED EACH OTHER

Long ago the raven and the owl lived happily as friends. Together they went out looking for food, shared everything they had fairly between them and knew no want. They lived many a long year, till their feathers turned whiter than snow.

One day the owl said to the raven:

"We've grown old without ever knowing what it is to be beautiful. All the other birds are decked out in red, black and grey, while you and I only show up during the short summer."

"That's quite right," said the raven.

"I know, why don't we paint each other," the owl suggested. "First you paint me, than I'll paint you."

The raven agreed. He took some charred blubber from a lamp, plucked a feather from his tail, and told the owl to prepare herself.

The owl perched on a stone, and the raven started carefully painting her as he moved around the stone, drawing beautiful black spots on each feather.

While he was painting the owl, the raven thought: "Now I'll try and make a real beauty out of her. She'll see what a fine piece of work this is and will make me beautiful as well."

The raven spent quite a long time doing his best to paint the owl. The owl grew tired of sitting still on the stone, and thought: "The raven has been plaguing the life out of me, to be sure. When my turn comes, I'll paint him in a jiffy."

At long last the raven finished his handiwork and said:

"Look, how beautiful I've made you! Now dry out a little in the wind and then paint me, too."

The owl agreed. After drying herself in the wind, she told the raven to prepare himself.

The raven perched on the stone, but the owl said:

"Oh no, stand here next to the stone, for I'll paint you in a different way. Close your eyes, and open them only when I tell you."

The raven stood by the stone, shut his eyes, and got ready. The owl took the lamp with the charred blubber, clambered up onto the stone, and poured the blubber over the raven from head to tail. The raven turned black in a trice.

"Now dry out a little in the wind," said the owl, "and then open your eyes and look at yourself. Although I painted you quickly, now everyone will see you come winter come summer."

The raven dried in the wind, opened his eyes and screamed:

"Oh my, what have you done?! Every little rabbit and mouse will see me coming. How am I supposed to find food now?"

To this the owl replied:

"But you yourself wanted to be beautiful!"

This made the raven angrier than ever.

"I tried my hardest when I painted you!" he said. "Now you're a real beauty, but I'm black as soot because of you. Get out of my sight, owl! I never want to see you again!"

The owl grew frightened and flew away.

From that time on, the raven has been black and the owl speckled. The owl always tries to avoid the raven, because she's afraid of him.

THE EIDER DUCKS AND THE FOX

Once upon a time the sly fox was walking along the seashore thinking to himself: "There's no animal brighter than me, nor any animal slyer!"

Just then some eider ducks swam by in the sea. They saw the fox and decided to trick him. Said the chief duck:

"You know, brothers, let's make a boat from our wings. We'll line up two by two with our wing tips touching. The fox will think it's a boat."

No sooner said than done. They lined up in two rows and spread out their wings. The middle looked like a boat with winged oars on either side. As the ducks skimmed across the sea, their leader shouted:

"Heave-ho, heave-ho! In out, in out, lively does it, lads!"

The fox's eyes had grown dim with the years. He looked out to sea and saw a boat with oarsmen in it, lustily heaving away. The fox stopped and shouted:

"Ahoy! Oarsmen, put in to shore and give me a ride! Don't you see who's walking along the shore? It's me, the master in these parts! Can't you see I'm tired!"

The eider ducks swam over to the shore. The fox climbed right into the middle of the little boat. He sat down, proudly puffed out his chest,

7

unfurled his tail, and smiled with delight. The boat quickly sailed away from the shore.

Suddenly the fox heard the voice of the ducks' leader:

"Well, brothers, we've had a good swim, so let's fly off now!"

Before the fox had time to come to his senses, he was dropped into the water. When he looked around, the ducks were already far away.

The fox started to swim toward the shore. As he swam, he thought: "Oh, did those ducks fool me. They disgraced me before the whole world."

It was hard for the fox to swim, because his drenched tail was pulling him down to the bottom.

"My tail, my beauty," the fox implored, "don't let me down, help me swim to safety!"

His tail started to steer him to the shore.

The fox barely reached dry land; he crawled onto a hillock and started to dry out in the sun.

In the meantime, the eider ducks flew over the whole tundra and told everyone how the fox had taken a dip in the sea.

Soon afterwards, all the animals, large and small, gathered round the fox to look at him and have a good laugh:

"Could you please tell us, dear fox, how the eider ducks managed to give you a freezing dip in the sea?"

At this the fox jumped up, shook himself, grabbed his wet tail in his teeth to make it easier for him to run, and bolted into the tundra to hide his shame. And the fox has never walked by the seashore to this day.

THE SINGING RABBIT

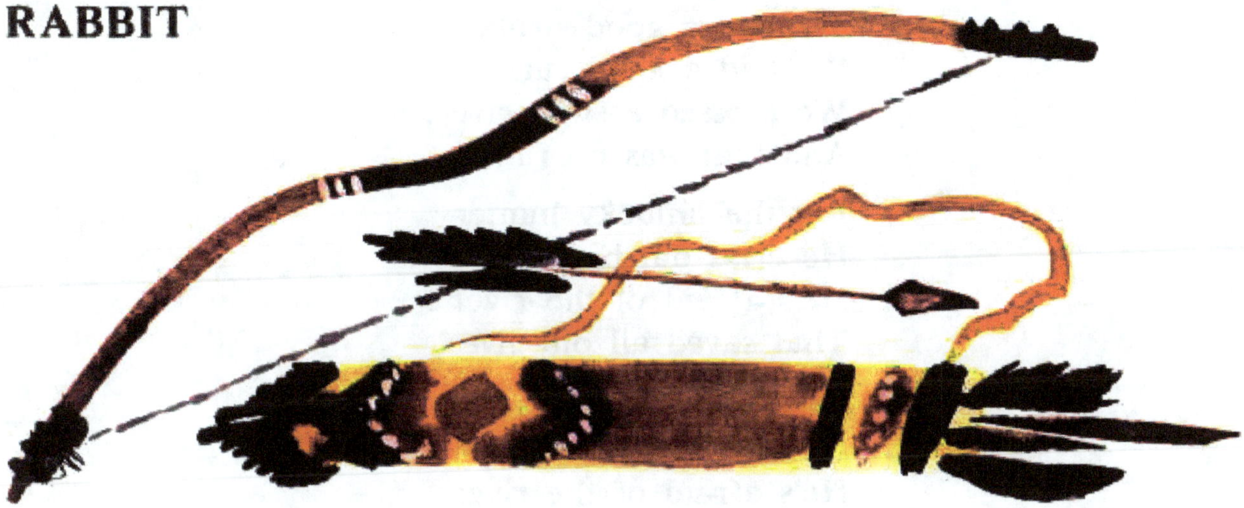

Once upon a time a young hunter went into the tundra to try his luck. He carried a bow in his hand, and a quiver with sharp-pointed arrows hung from his belt. As he walked on and on, he saw a rabbit with her little ones. Quietly he started sneaking up behind them, but the mother-rabbit saw the hunter and cried:

"Quick, my children, follow me!"

And the little bunnies hopped off after their mother.

The hunter started to chase them. He ran and ran for a long time and almost caught up with them when suddenly he saw a fast-flowing river before him.

The rabbits jumped into the river one by one.

By the time he reached the river, the rabbits had swum to the opposite shore and hidden themselves behind a little hill.

The hunter stopped down to the water. The river flowed so swiftly and was so deep, that he could not even see the bottom. No, it was impossible for him to cross it.

Sad and angry, the hunter sat down on a stone and wept bitterly.

The smallest of the bunnies stuck his long ears out from behind the hill and started to sing ditty to annoy the hunter:

We had a good stroll,
We had a good run,
We crossed a swift river,
And that was no fun!

But the unlucky hunter
He cries out his eyes —
He's afraid of the river
That saved all our lives!

Hi-hi-hi, ha-ha-ha
Ho-ho-ho, ha-ha-ha
He's afraid of the river
That saved our lives!

That was how the naughty bunny sang at him!

There was nothing for the unlucky hunter to do but put his arrows back into his quiver and set off for home empty-handed.

Angrily he brandished his bow at the little rabbits saying:

"Just you wait, little bunnies! You shan't fool me next time!"

Y. CHARUSHIN

WHY TUPPY DOESN'T CHASE BIRDS

HOW TUPPY GOT HIS NAME

When Tuppy is surprised or sees something strange he makes a funny tup-tup-tup sound with his lips.

When the wind blows in the grass, when a bird flies by or a butterfly flutters its wings, Tuppy creeps up to it with his eyes wide open, saying, "Tup-tup-tup, I'll catch you! I'll pounce on you! I'll play with you!"

And that's how Tuppy got his name.

Once Tuppy heard a soft whistle.

There in the gooseberry bushes were quick little grey birds hunting for bugs and beetles.

Tuppy crept up softly and hid. He held his breath. He didn't even say tup-tup-tup, because he was afraid he'd scare the birds away. Suddenly, he pounced on them! He nearly caught one. But he didn't.

Tuppy did not know how to catch birds. He was only a little kitten.

MOTHER CAT THINKS TUPPY IS STILL A BABY

One day Tuppy got a spanking. It was Netty, his mother, who spanked him. Cats always chase their big kittens away when they have little ones, but her little ones had been given away. The next day she miaowed and purred and called to him. Tuppy remembered his spanking. He didn't come to her. He didn't want to get spanked again.

Netty purred: "Come here, silly."

Tuppy licked his chops. He had learned how to drink milk from a saucer, but Netty's milk was much tastier.

Finally, he crept over to her. Soon he was fast asleep.

Then strange things began to happen.

After all, Tuppy was growing up. But Netty felt he was still a tiny baby. So she rolled him over and began to lick and wash him.

Tuppy woke up in surprise. He didn't like his washing. He could wash himself.

He wanted to scramble off, but Netty purred: "Lie still, you're a tiny baby, you'll get lost if you run away."

She purred and purred until she finally fell asleep herself.

Then Tuppy climbed out of the basket and went off to have some fun.

He was going to catch butterflies and pounce on a sparrow.

When Netty woke up she saw that her darling little Tuppy was gone. He was lost!

She ran out into the yard and called to him.

There he was, on the roof, running about after the sparrows.

Netty rushed up to him.

“Be careful! You’ll fall!” she warned.

But Tuppy didn’t even listen. So Netty took him by the scruff of his neck and carried him down, just as if he were a tiny baby. Tuppy kicked and squealed. He wanted to play on the roof.

Once Netty had him back in the basket she washed him and purred. She could not understand that Tuppy was a big kitten and did not need a nanny any more.

WHY TUPPY DOESN'T CHASE BIRDS

One day Tuppy saw a sparrow sitting on a branch singing a song. "Chirp, chirp!" sang the sparrow.

"Tup-tup-tup! I'll catch you! I'll pounce on you! I'll play with you!" Tuppy said and crept closer.

But the sparrow saw him. It chirped still louder. "Look, there's a cat here! See where he's hiding! There he is!"

And suddenly sparrows came flying down from everywhere. They sat on the bushes and branches. Some even landed right in front of Tuppy

And they all began to scold: "Chirp, chirp! Chirp, chirp!"

The noise was enough to make you deaf.

Tuppy became frightened. He had never heard such a racket. And ran off as fast as he could.

The sparrows kept right on scolding Tuppy. Then they told each other how brave they had been to scare away a cat.

There was no one for Tuppy to catch. No one wanted to be caught. So Tuppy climbed a tree and hid among the branches.

He looked this way and that, but he couldn't see any birds. They could see him, though. They had been watching him.

Then Tuppy saw them. Strange-looking birds were staring at him. These weren't little grey birds or scolding sparrows. These were nearly as big as he was, they were big blackbirds, looking for a tree in which to build their nest.

He looked very strange to them, too.

Tuppy was very pleased. "Tup-tup-tup! Who can they be? Tup-tup-tup! I'll catch you! I'll pounce on you! I'll play with you!"

But Tuppy didn't know which one to catch first.

One big blackbird was sitting in back of him. The other was in front, and very close.

Tuppy looked this way and that. First at one, then at the other. While he was looking at the one in back, the one in front pecked him. That hurt. Tuppy couldn't understand who had pecked him.

He jumped off the tree and ran into the bushes.

And now, whenever he sees a bird, Tuppy never pays any attention to it. He doesn't chase birds any more.

www.ingramcontent.com/pod-product-compliance
Lightning Source LLC
LaVergne TN
LVHW062123171026
850499LV00045B/2000

Visiting Grandpa
N. Nosov
Translated from the Russian by *Fainna Solasko*
Drawings by *I Semenov*

The Singing Rabbit
Eskimo Folk Tales
Adapted for Children by *G Menovshchikov*
Translated by *Anatoly Bilenko*
Drawings by *Tatyana Chursinova*

Why Tuppy Doesn't Chase Birds
Y Charushin

ISBN 978-93-90355-61-7
9 789390 355617 >
children's literature
www.insightpublica.com
facebook.com/insightpublica
INSIGHT PUBLICA